TEEN TITANS GO!™

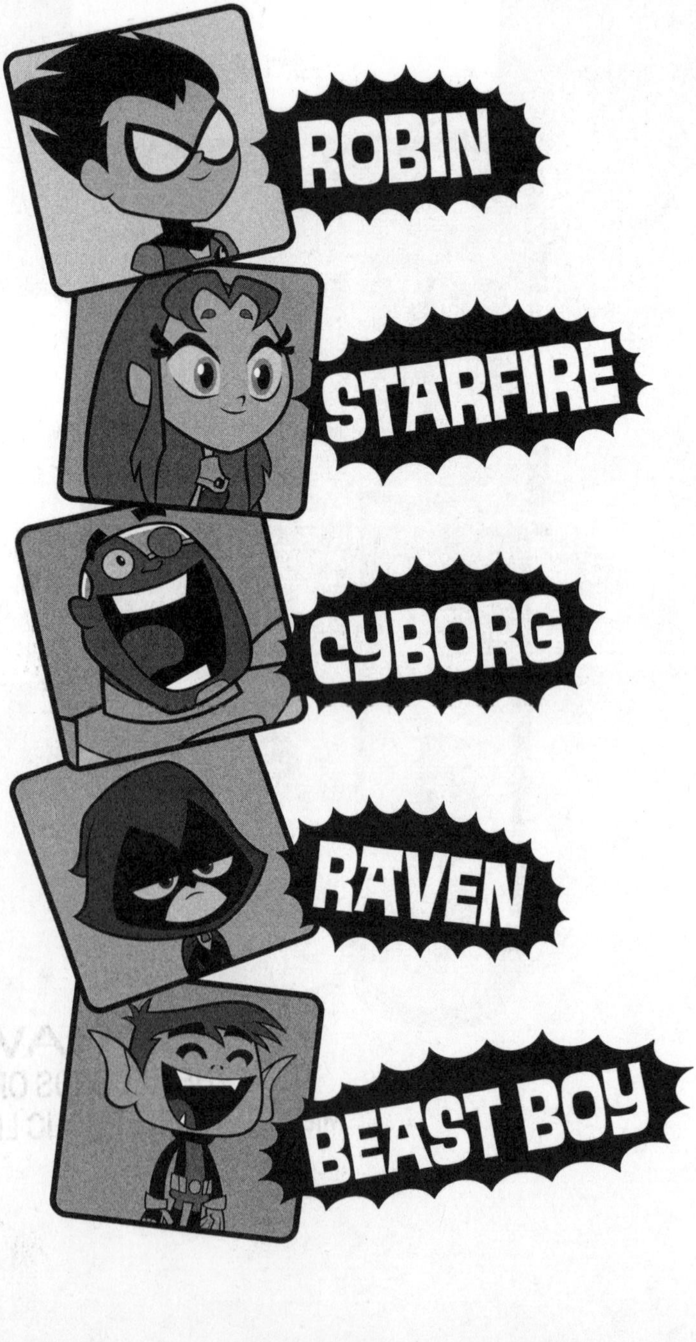
ROBIN
STARFIRE
CYBORG
RAVEN
BEAST BOY

BEAST BOY BRO-DOWN

Adapted by **Steve Korté**
Based on the episodes
"Nature" by **Merrill Hagan**
"Man-Person" by **Merrill Hagan**
and
"BBBDAY!" by **Ben Gruber**

LITTLE, BROWN AND COMPANY
New York   Boston

Copyright © 2016 DC Comics.
TEEN TITANS GO! and all related characters and elements are trademarks of and © DC Comics.
(s16)

Little, Brown and Company

Hachette Book Group
1290 Avenue of the Americas, New York, NY 10104
Visit us at lb-kids.com

Little, Brown and Company is a division of Hachette Book Group, Inc.
The Little, Brown name and logo are trademarks of Hachette Book Group, Inc.

The publisher is not responsible for websites (or their content)
that are not owned by the publisher.

First Edition: May 2016

Library of Congress Control Number: 2015954822

ISBN: 978-0-316-26747-2

10 9 8 7 6 5 4 3 2 1

RRD-C

Printed in the United States of America

CONTENTS

Nature 1

Man-Person 41

BBBDAY! 91

Bonus Activity 134

NATURE

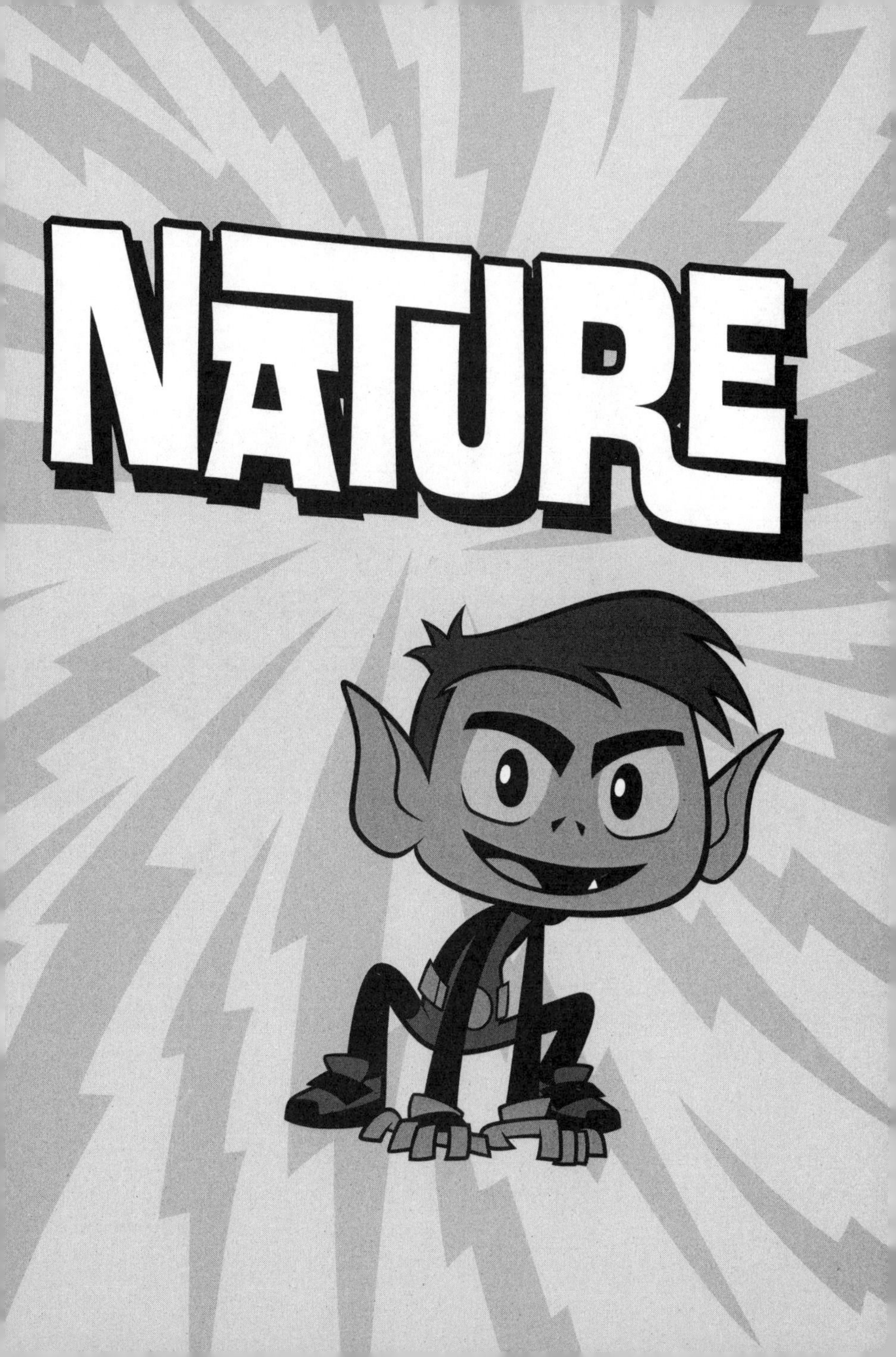

CHAPTER 1

"Eeek! Help us!" the citizens of Jump City cried as a giant monster rampaged through the streets, crushing cars and knocking over buildings.

On a nearby rooftop, the Teen Titans quickly gathered and prepared for battle with the evil beast.

"Star and Raven, you two take the left flank,"

called out Robin. "Cyborg and I will take the right!"

Robin turned to Beast Boy, who was eagerly jumping from one foot to the other.

"Beast Boy," said Robin, "I want you to go pterodactyl right up the middle!"

"You got it, Rob!" Beast Boy said enthusiastically.

"Okay! Teen Titans, go!" yelled Robin.

With that command, Starfire and Raven flew toward the monster.

4

Cyborg transformed himself into a jetpack and launched into the air, with Robin holding on to him tightly. Beast Boy jumped off the ledge of the building and sailed through the air, ready to change into a fierce pterodactyl!

Seconds later, he crashed to the ground, still in his original Beast Boy form.

"Whoa!" he said woozily. "What happened to my pterodactyl?"

Above him, the Teen Titans were battling the monster.

"Hurry up, Beastie," called out Cyborg. "We need you!"

"It's cheetah time!" yelled Beast Boy. He started running faster and faster, heading toward the monster and getting ready to turn into a savage cheetah.

Blam!

Beast Boy slammed into one leg of the monster. He had failed to transform again.

As Raven zapped the monster with her dark magic, she looked down at Beast Boy with concern.

"Uh, is there something wrong with your powers?" she asked.

Beast Boy glared at her as he rubbed his aching head and quickly said, "Of course not!"

Robin yelled down to Beast Boy, "Glad to hear it, because we need a rhino to knock this guy off balance!"

"One rhino coming at you!" Beast Boy declared. He narrowed his eyes, used all his concentration to imagine a giant rhino horn on his forehead, and with a loud yell charged at the monster as...

...Beast Boy.

Just then, the monster raised one of its legs and kicked Beast Boy, sending him flying through the air. Beast Boy slammed into a lamppost, which cracked in two and landed with a thud on top of the monster. The creature was knocked unconscious.

"*That's* how rhinos do it!" declared Beast Boy as he jumped from foot to foot in a victory dance.

The other Titans looked at one another doubtfully.

CHAPTER 2

Back at Titans Tower, Beast Boy's team-mates gathered around him.

"Admit it, Beast Boy," said Robin. "You've lost your powers."

"No way, bro," said Beast Boy as he walked away. "I was just having an off day."

Raven flew in front of him and said, "Beast Boy, we need to talk about this."

"Okay," he agreed. "We can talk about it

over the vegan portabella pizza with creamy truffle sauce that I've prepared. But first I need to chill our glasses to forty-four degrees for the sparkling apple cider. I added just a hint of nutmeg to the cider to make it more assertive."

As the Titans gathered around the dinner table, they were surprised to see that Beast Boy had set the table with fine china dinner plates, gleaming silverware, and a linen tablecloth. There were even place cards to tell each Titan where to sit.

"Oooh, highly delicious looking!" said Starfire as Beast Boy eased the steaming-hot pizza onto a crystal serving tray. Cyborg reached out to grab a slice of pizza.

"Ouch!" he cried when Beast Boy smacked his hand with a spatula.

"Were you just gonna eat that with your hands, bro? Gross!" said Beast Boy. "Use a serving fork."

"A serving *what*?" asked Cyborg, completely confused.

Beast Boy turned to Starfire and said, "Would you mind chewing a bit more quietly? And, Robin, please wipe your mouth with your napkin, not your glove!"

"When did *Beast Boy* become the civilized one?" Raven asked with surprise.

"That's it!" declared Robin. "That's the problem! The comforts of modern living have stripped Beast Boy of his animal instincts!"

"Then that is why he cannot turn into the animals," said Starfire.

Beast Boy started freaking out and jumped back from the table. "You're right!" he said. "The old Beast Boy would never have used a serving fork to eat pizza! The only way I can get my powers back is to reconnect with Mother Nature!"

Robin reached out to grab his teammate.

"Be careful, Beast Boy," he said. "She is the *worst* mother of all. There's a reason we all live inside."

But Beast Boy broke away and quickly ripped off his uniform.

"I got to do it, bro!" he yelled as he ran out the door, wearing just his white briefs. "I got to run free!"

The four Titans looked at one another and smiled.

"More pizza for us!" declared Cyborg. They all resumed eating.

CHAPTER 3

Beast Boy scampered through a beautiful forest, his arms outstretched and a big smile on his face.

"Finally! Back to Mother Nature!" he called out. "Beautiful sun! Fresh air! Clean water!"

He paused in front of a small lake and scooped up a handful of water.

"So good, so fresh, so…" he said happily as he slurped down the water. "Yuck! So hairy!"

He gagged, pulling a clump of brown fur out of his mouth.

Nearby, a giant brown grizzly bear glared at Beast Boy. The bear had been cleaning itself, sending huge balls of fur into the water.

"No problem," said Beast Boy as he walked into the forest. Just then, a tiny bug landed on his shoulder.

"What's up, buggy bug?" asked Beast Boy. "How's nature been treating you, baby?"

The bug didn't answer. Instead, it slithered into Beast Boy's ear!

"Ack! Bug in my ear! Get out! Get out! Get out!" cried Beast Boy.

To his relief, the bug emerged from his other ear. Then it crawled up Beast Boy's nose!

"Even worse! It tickles! Get out!" yelled Beast Boy.

He then grabbed a branch off a nearby tree and brought it down sharply on his own head. The bug popped out of his mouth.

Beast Boy wearily sat down on a log. A long green snake slithered up next to him.

"Yo, snake-dude, good to see you," said Beast Boy. "You wouldn't believe the day I'm having out here in the—"

Before he could finish his sentence, the snake jumped up and bit Beast Boy's nose.

"Owwwwww!" screamed Beast Boy as he jumped off the log and ran back to the lake.

Smack!

He collided with the grizzly bear, which let out a loud roar and chased Beast Boy back into the forest.

"Worst day in nature *ever*!" yelled Beast Boy as he ran from the bear.

CHAPTER 4

After three weeks, Beast Boy had not returned to Titans Tower, so his teammates decided to search for him in the forest.

"I *warned* Beast Boy about coming into this hostile environment," Robin said as they walked cautiously through the woods. "We just need to remember that Mother Nature is against us out here. We will have to do whatever it takes to survive until we find Beast Boy."

"I just hope he's alive when we find him!" added Cyborg.

"Of course he will be alive," said Starfire. "Because if he is not, the animals will have surely scattered his remains across the forest, leaving no trace for us to find!"

"Way to look on the bright side, Star," said Raven with a sigh.

A butterfly floated by Robin, and the Boy Wonder quickly grabbed it and popped the insect into his mouth.

Gulp!

"Eeeew! What did you do that for?" asked Cyborg with dismay.

"Pure protein," explained Robin. "Out here in the wild you have to take every meal you can get. You never know when you'll have a chance to eat again."

"Um, crazy boy, you just ate a *sandwich* five minutes ago!" said Raven.

Gulp!

Robin swallowed another butterfly.

"Robin! *Please* stop doing that!" implored Starfire.

21

"Pure protein!" said Robin before he let out
a gentle burp.

In another part of the forest, far away
from the other Teen Titans, sat a very dejected
Beast Boy. He was wearing just his underwear
and shivering in the cold.

"Man, I wish I hadn't torn off my uniform,"
he grumbled to himself. "I'm freezing, and

I'm hungry. I sure could use something warm to eat."

Just then, a plump and fuzzy rabbit hopped up and cuddled next to him.

"Hey, bunny," said Beast Boy. "Wow, how do you stay so meaty, bro? I mean, look at your delicious, thick thighs. And that soft, warm fur of yours would make an *awesome* sweater!"

The rabbit looked nervously at Beast Boy.

Beast Boy licked his lips and then lunged for the rabbit, which ran away in alarm.

"Come back, bunny!" Beast Boy called as he ran after the rabbit. "Let me put you in my mouth!"

The rabbit jumped through a giant bush with Beast Boy right behind it.

Crash!

Beast Boy slammed into a beautiful young woman who was floating above the ground and holding the rabbit in her arms. She was dressed in white, with tiny wings on her back and a glowing golden crown on top of her head. She looked down at Beast Boy with a smile.

"Whoa," he said. "Who are you?"

"I am Mother Nature," she replied.

"Well, that's my lunch, Mama!" declared Beast Boy as he reached for the rabbit.

Beast Boy and Mother Nature struggled for a minute, but then he dropped to the ground and started sobbing.

"What am I doing?" he cried. "This place is making me crazy! I almost ate that adorable bunny!"

Beast Boy looked up and noticed with surprise

that the rabbit was no longer in her arms.

"Hey, where did the bunny go?" he asked.

"He's right over there," Mother Nature said, pointing to the giant grizzly bear that had just gulped down the rabbit in one tasty bite.

Beast Boy gasped and said, "Robin was right! You *are* the worst mother ever! How could you let that bear eat the bunny?"

"I preach survival of the fittest here," she explained. "One animal eats another. It's the circle of life."

Beast Boy was not convinced.

"You don't need any circles if you have taco stands!" he declared.

Mother Nature was intrigued and said, "Taco? Can you explain this taco to me?"

"No problem, Mama," Beast Boy replied with a smile. "Tacos are *exactly* what this place needs!"

CHAPTER 5

Deep in the forest, the other members of the Teen Titans continued their search for Beast Boy. Robin had stripped down to tiny green shorts and covered his body with green camouflage paint in an attempt to disguise himself as a leafy bush.

"Interesting new look, Robin," said Raven sarcastically.

"If Mother Nature wants to attack me,

she's going to have to find me first!" he said smugly. He then fell to his knees and started sniffing the ground.

"Titans, I have discovered Beast Boy's trail!" he declared. "Follow me!"

Robin led his teammates deeper into the woods, where they came upon a pile of bones on the floor of the forest, next to a bush covered with plump red berries.

Robin stuffed a handful of berries into his mouth and said between gulps, "I know exactly what happened to Beast Boy!"

"And I know those berries are definitely poisonous, and you should stop eating them," said Raven.

Ignoring her as he ate more berries, Robin continued, "Beast Boy regained his instincts and was able to turn into animals again!"

28

Starfire clapped her hands in delight. "That is the great news!" she said happily.

Robin swallowed more berries and added, "But then Beast Boy got cocky. Prancing through the forest in the form of a deer, he had a fateful meeting with the majestic King

Deer! They couldn't come to terms, so Beast Boy challenged him to become the emperor of the forest. It's all so very clear now!"

"Those berries are going to your head, dude," said Cyborg.

"I do not understand," said Starfire. "Where is Beast Boy now?"

Robin pointed to the pile of bones on the ground and said dramatically, "*This* is Beast Boy!"

"No, that's not him," Raven said with a shake of her head.

"Poor, poor Beast Boy!" wailed Robin. "You could never be emperor of the forest! Couldn't you see that? Why did you challenge King Deer for his throne? You were just a boy! Just a boy!" He fell to the ground, sobbing.

"Um, Robin," said Raven. "That's not the

skeleton of a deer. That's a moose. And there is no such thing as King Deer."

Robin jumped up and said, "Well, that's a relief! Come on, Titans. Our search continues!"

As they continued walking, Cyborg wiped his brow. "All this searching sure is hot work," he said. "I could use something cold to drink."

"I could also use the liquid refreshment," agreed Starfire.

"Here you go, Star," said Robin. He reached into his backpack and handed her a canteen. She happily started drinking and then gave the canteen to Cyborg and Raven, who each took long swigs of water.

Cyborg licked his lips and looked suspiciously at Robin. "Where did that water come from?" he asked. "From that dirty lake with all those fish swimming in it?"

"It's clean," Robin declared. "It came from me."

Raven looked up, surprised. "Yeah, but where did you get it?"

"I made it," Robin said with exasperation. "*It came from me!*"

Cyborg, Raven, and Starfire stared at

Robin in horror and simultaneously spit out the water.

"Please tell me that wasn't what I *think* it was!" yelled Cyborg.

"It was distilled, purified, and filtered four times," Robin said with annoyance. "We have to do what we have to do to survive in the wild!"

Just then, a butterfly drifted by. Robin

jumped in the air, snatched it, and gobbled it down.

"Pure protein!" he yelled with a laugh, and went running deeper into the woods.

Raven looked disgusted. "I am *so* ready to go back to the Tower," she said.

In another part of the forest, Mother Nature and Beast Boy were standing in front of a beautiful glade with a tiny pond that was surrounded by tall pine trees.

"This is the perfect place for our taco stands," declared Beast Boy.

"Are you *sure* that these taco stands will improve the forest?" she asked doubtfully.

"I guarantee it, Big Mama," he said. "But first, you gotta ditch most of these trees."

Mother Nature hesitated for a moment, but then she shrugged and raised her right hand.

"Well, okay," she said.

Zap!

All the trees at the edge of the glade magically disappeared. Beast Boy was delighted.

"See how that opens everything up?" he asked. "Now for some real estate. You need to put some buildings in there."

Mother Nature waved her hand again.

Poof!

A row of bushes disappeared and was replaced by dozens of homes and skyscrapers.

"Now we're cookin'!" Beast Boy said happily. "And speaking of cookin', let's get some of those taco stands in here."

"*Bueno!*" said Mother Nature with a wave.

Crackle!

The pond was magically transformed into a giant taco stand. All the fish in the pond were changed into fish tacos!

"Now some billboards to advertise the taco stand," said Beast Boy. "And more buildings. Lots more buildings!"

By the time she was done, not a trace of the forest around them remained.

"Maybe some air-conditioning?" asked Mother Nature eagerly.

"That's a no-brainer!" agreed Beast Boy.

The two of them surveyed the scene. All the animals were peacefully lined up at the taco stand, waiting patiently to order their fish tacos.

"Look at that!" said Beast Boy with satisfaction. "No one's eating anyone. Well, except for the fish in the tacos, I guess. Everyone's got their own home *and* air-conditioning! That's what I call nature!"

"This is *so* much better, Beast Boy," said Mother Nature. "How can I ever thank you?"

She reached down to embrace Beast Boy and hugged him tightly to her.

Pop!

Beast Boy suddenly transformed himself into a happy green rabbit.

"Look!" he yelled happily. "I reconnected with nature. Literally! Yo, my powers are back!"

Pop! Pop! Pop!

Beast Boy rapidly transformed himself into a bear. Then a wolf. Then a Maine coon cat.

"That's what I'm talking about," he purred.

Pop!

Beast Boy turned himself into a green butterfly.

"Oh yeah, I'm back—" he started to say just as Robin and the other Titans arrived.

Before Beast Boy could finish his sentence, Robin's hand darted out, grabbed the butterfly, and popped it into his mouth.

38

Gulp!

"Pure protein!" he declared happily, then looked around. "Hey, where is Beast Boy?"

"I'm pretty sure that was Beast Boy you just swallowed," said Cyborg.

"Ewww, spit him out!" said Raven.

"No way!" said Robin. "Pure protein!"

MAN-PERSON

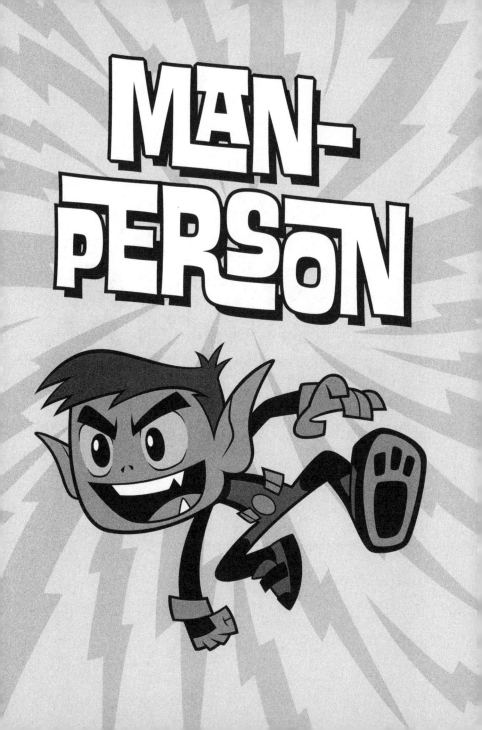

CHAPTER

1

It was another day in Jump City and another robot was crashing through the streets. This one was over one hundred feet tall, with four long arms that smashed into buildings and toppled automobiles. Fortunately, the Teen Titans were on the scene.

"Teen Titans, go!" called out Robin.

Beast Boy jumped in front of his teammates

and declared, "This one is *mine*, bro!"

Pop!

Beast Boy transformed into a ferocious green gorilla and charged at the robot. Seconds later, the robot slammed one of its giant fists right into Beast Boy's face.

"Owwwwwwwwwwwwww!" yelled Beast Boy as he crashed to the ground. His teammates noticed with concern that the robot's fist was still attached to Beast Boy's face.

"Ow, ow, ow," Beast Boy groaned on the sidewalk.

"Yeah, that's gonna hurt tomorrow," observed Raven.

One hour later, in a private room at Jump City Hospital, the Teen Titans gathered around Beast Boy's bed. The robot's fist was still wedged into Beast Boy's face!

"Stay with us, Beast Boy!" Robin called out to his friend. "We are *not* going to lose you today!"

Robin then turned to Raven and said, "I need a bone saw!"

Poof!

Raven magically created a bone saw, which Robin used to hack off big chunks of the robot's hand.

Raven then created pliers, which Robin used to pry off the last bits of the fist.

"Foreign object removed!" Robin said triumphantly, tossing the shards of metallic hand onto the floor.

Beast Boy quickly raised his hands to cover his battle-scarred face.

"Oh, man! My face! My beautiful face," he whimpered.

"Stay calm, Beastie," said Cyborg. "We've all had battle wounds. Let's see how bad it is."

Beast Boy slowly lowered his hands.

"Eeeeeeew!" cried out his teammates. "Cover it up! Cover it up!"

"Bandages! We need bandages!" yelled Robin.

Raven magically created bandages that quickly encircled Beast Boy's entire head.

"It's just going to take a little while to heal," Robin said reassuringly to Beast Boy.

Cyborg, Raven, and Starfire all looked doubtfully at Robin.

Six weeks later, at Titans Tower, a still-bandaged Beast Boy sat up in bed as his teammates gathered around him.

"All right, Beast Boy," said Robin. "Let's see how you're healing under there."

The bandages were removed. And the Titans screamed again.

"Eeek! His face! I cannot look at his face!" cried Starfire.

"Wow, gross!" observed Raven.

Blorg! went Cyborg as he threw up.

"Cover him up! Cover him up!" yelled Robin as new bandages were wrapped around Beast Boy's face.

"See you in six weeks, Beast Boy," said his teammates, and they left the room.

CHAPTER 2

Another six weeks later, the Teen Titans again stood next to Beast Boy's bed.

"Okay, time to take off the bandages," said Robin as the other Titans looked on nervously.

When the last bandage was removed from Beast Boy's face, the other four Titans gasped.

"You're finally healed, Beastie!" said Cyborg.

"Yeah, but how does it look?" demanded Beast Boy.

There was silence from his teammates.

Raven and Starfire glanced at each other nervously. Robin looked the other way while he rolled up the bandages. Cyborg was busy polishing a scratch on his armor.

Beast Boy frowned and grabbed a mirror. He then let out a moan when he looked at his face and saw the jagged red scar that started on his forehead and descended below his right eye.

"Oh, man!" he cried. "This scar is *huge*!"

Pop! Pop! Pop!

Beast Boy rapidly transformed into an elephant, then an ocelot, and then a puma. All three animals had the same jagged scar on their faces.

"My beautiful face—it's ruined!" he wailed.

Cyborg tried to reassure him. "C'mon, bro. It's not *that* bad. Right, guys?"

"Well, um…" said Raven. Robin and Starfire were silent.

Cyborg glared at them and then said to Beast Boy, "Well, I think it makes you look *tough*!"

Beast Boy replied in a sulky voice, "Yeah, right…"

Cyborg put his hand on Beast Boy's shoulder and said, "I'm serious! Who's the toughest person you know?"

Beast Boy considered this question for a moment and then answered, "Raven."

"Wow, really?" said Raven with a smile. "Cool!"

Cyborg looked annoyed. "No, I mean, who's the toughest *man*-person you know?"

Beast Boy looked up at Cyborg and said, "*You're* the toughest man-person I know."

Cyborg quickly stuck his tongue out at Raven, then continued, "Bro, do you think I started out that way? No! I used to be an average-looking dude, minding my own business, until my body got all messed up in a crazy accident. My papa hooked me up with all these robot parts, and after that I got a few scars of my own. Those scars are what make me tough!"

Starfire nodded in agreement and said, "On my planet, one is not a true warrior until he or she has earned scars from victories."

"For reals?" asked Beast Boy doubtfully.

"Yes. For the reals, Beast Boy," she said.

Raven moved closer and said, "And I think it makes you look…"

She paused. Beast Boy's eyes widened.

"Yes? It makes me look…it makes me look…?" he questioned.

Raven sighed and then said reluctantly, "…manly."

Beast Boy's face lit up with a wide smile.

"It *is* a pretty rad scar, Beast Boy," admitted Robin.

Pop!

Suddenly, Beast Boy changed into a tall green ostrich and grabbed the mirror again.

Studying his feathered face, he said, "Hey, what's up with that ostrich? Why is he so manly? Oh, it's just the rad scar on his *face*!"

Beast Boy jumped out of bed and swaggered over to Cyborg.

"C'mon, dude!" Beast Boy said. "Wanna go and be tough?"

"You know it, Beastie!" said Cyborg with a grin. "Something tells me that we've got some tough times ahead of us!"

CHAPTER

3

And so began the tough times of Beast Boy and Cyborg. The two of them soon became more inseparable.

When Cyborg lifted a barbell weighing three hundred fifty pounds, Beast Boy was on a bench right next to him, straining to lift a fifty-pound barbell. When Cyborg wore a leather jacket, Beast Boy donned a leather vest. When Cyborg grabbed an electric guitar and played a blistering guitar solo, Beast Boy strapped on a bass guitar and hit deep, rumbling notes that shook the walls of Titans Tower.

One night at the dinner table, Robin reached for the last slice of pizza, but he quickly drew back his hand when Cyborg started growling at him.

Cyborg then grabbed the slice of pizza, cut it in half, and shared it with Beast Boy.

"Tough dudes gotta tough it out together,"

said Cyborg, as he and Beast Boy happily munched on their pizza.

After two weeks of toughness, Cyborg and Beast Boy were relaxing in the living room, playing video games and seeing who could burp the loudest. Suddenly, Robin burst into the room.

"Dr. Light is on a rampage downtown!" he yelled. "Titans, go!"

The team rushed out of Titans Tower. They quickly surrounded the villain Dr. Light, who had the power to blast dangerous light rays from his fingers. He was standing in the middle of a busy intersection with his hands extended, zapping cars and lampposts with blinding-white rays of light.

"One tough cheetah coming up!" said Beast Boy with a smile.

Pop!

A scar-faced green cheetah charged at Dr. Light and knocked the villain off balance. A laser ray erupted from Dr. Light's hand and zapped a nearby building, slicing into it!

The Titans looked up in dismay as a giant chunk of the building came loose with a horrible screeching sound. Soon, it toppled over and came crashing down toward them.

"Got it!" yelled Cyborg. With one hand, he easily caught the falling debris and saved the Titans.

"Whoa, that was super-tough!" said Beast Boy with awe.

Cyborg smiled as he tossed the wreckage aside and then flexed his metal bicep and said, "Thank the scars, Beastie!"

Zap!

Dr. Light was still shooting rays at them. While his teammates jumped back into the battle, Beast Boy had an idea. Just as his teammates wrestled Dr. Light to the ground, one more beam shot above Beast Boy's head. As fast as he could, Beast Boy jumped up in the air with his left arm extended.

Pow!

Beast Boy's left hand was hit directly by Dr. Light's blast! Suddenly, there was no longer a hand at the end of Beast Boy's arm!

CHAPTER 4

After Dr. Light was turned over to the police, the Titans gathered around Beast Boy in the Titans Tower living room.

"Beast Boy, your hand...it is gone," said Starfire with concern. "Are you feeling well?"

"Never better, Star!" said Beast Boy with a grin as he extended his left arm and marveled at his missing hand. "How cool is this?"

"Don't worry, Beast Boy," said Robin, who was carrying a small glass container. "I've got your left hand in this jar. We just need to figure out a way to reattach it to your arm."

As Robin said that, the hand in the jar kept changing forms, from hoof to paw to claw.

"You're lucky that your animal superpowers are keeping your hand alive," observed Robin.

"That's *so* gross," said Raven.

"I got this, Beastie," said Cyborg as he grabbed a toolbox and crouched down in front of his teammate. With pliers, screws, a welding gun, and chunks of metal, Cyborg quickly fashioned a robotic hand and attached it to the end of Beast Boy's left arm.

"Okay, Beast Bud," said Cyborg, "this should help you adjust until we figure out how to reattach your hand."

Beast Boy couldn't believe it. He held his left arm in the air and flexed the fingers on his new, shiny, immense cyborg hand.

"Don't worry, Beast Boy," said Robin. "It's going to be okay."

"Okay, dude? Are you kidding?" replied Beast Boy. "It's going to be *awesome!*"

"Are you not upset with the loss of your appendage?" asked Starfire with surprise.

"Why would I be upset?" said Beast Boy. "I now have this sweet robot hand to go with my manly scar!"

Pop!

Beast Boy transformed into a giant green grizzly bear and reared up on his hind legs, proudly roaring, as he displayed his robotic hand and fuzzy, scarred face.

"I have to admit, that is the coolest thing I've ever seen," said Robin.

"Amazing!" agreed Starfire.

In a quiet voice, Raven added, "So hot…"

Grizzly Beast Boy quickly jumped over and gave Raven a tight bear hug.

"What was that you said, Rae-Rae?" he asked.

Blam!

Raven knocked Beast Boy onto his back and glared at him. "*Nothing!*" she said.

Inside the jar, Beast Boy's left hand gave a thumbs-up.

"Check it out," said Beast Boy. "Even my old hand loves it!"

Cyborg was watching all this with dismay.

He turned to Beast Boy and said, "Listen, Beastie. Robot hands are tough and all, but losing body parts isn't a good idea!"

Beast Boy frowned at his friend and said, "It worked for you, dude!"

Robin pulled Beast Boy's original left hand out of the jar and said, "Maybe Cyborg's right. Let's see if we can reattach this hand so that you—"

Swoooooooosh!

Before Robin could finish his sentence, Beast Boy's former left hand jumped in the air and yanked up on Robin's underpants, giving the Boy Wonder a wedgie! Cyborg, Starfire, and Raven all laughed. Beast Boy looked grim.

"Beast Boy, you are not laughing at the hand's mockery of Robin?" asked Starfire.

Beast Boy's eyes narrowed and he grimaced to make his face look as tough as possible.

"Beast Boy would have thought that was funny," he said with a frown, "but I'm a man now. Call me Scar Man!"

Pop!

With that, Scar Man transformed into a giant bald eagle with a scarred, feathered face and a gleaming cyborg hand at the end of his left wing.

"Whoa," said Raven with quiet admiration. "*So* tough!"

CHAPTER 5

For the next week, Scar Man strutted through Titans Tower, enjoying his new life. Each time he walked by Raven, he winked at her. He always made sure to wink with his right eye, since that was the one bisected by his facial scar.

"So very tough," she had to admit.

Meanwhile, Robin and Cyborg labored in the medical lab. Robin was desperately trying to deep-freeze former Beast Boy's left hand by cramming it into a cryogenic tube. But the hand was fighting back. It transformed into a seal paw and slapped Robin in the face.

"Ow, quit it!" said Robin.

"What is it with Beast Boy getting his hand blown off on purpose?" said Cyborg with dismay. "I was just trying to cheer him up by telling him that scars were cool. But now Beast Boy has taken it too far!"

Raven floated by with a dreamy look on her face and said, "Not Beast Boy. His name is Scar Man."

Cyborg frowned and yelled after her, "His name is *Beast Boy*!"

"Did someone call me by my former name?" asked a voice from outside the lab. Suddenly, a large canvas bag came flying through the

door and landed on the table in front of
Robin. Cyborg and Robin viewed the bag
with dismay as it thrashed and jumped up
and down on the table.

"What in the world—" began Robin as he
cautiously opened the canvas bag.

"Eeeeek!" screamed both Robin and
Cyborg.

Inside the bag were assorted former body

parts of Beast Boy, including one eyeball, two legs, a right arm attached to a hand, and a left arm that was handless.

"What have you *done*, Beast Boy?" cried Cyborg with horror.

Clonk! Clonk!

Robin and Cyborg turned around and gasped with astonishment as a twelve-foot-tall robot marched into the lab. Atop the robot's massive body sat Scar Man's tiny green head. An eye-patch appeared over his left eye. The scar surrounding Scar Man's right eye seemed to glow as he glared at them.

"Don't sweat it, dudes," he told them. "They're just some lame body parts I'm not using anymore. I thought you might want to keep them on ice."

"Eeeew!" said Robin as he dropped the

canvas bag on the floor. Instantly, former Beast Boy's body parts jumped out of the bag and went scuttling out of the lab.

"Wait! Come back!" screamed Robin as he ran out the door to follow the body parts.

"Why did you do it, Beast Boy?" asked Cyborg sadly.

"Just decided to make myself a little tougher," Scar Man boasted. "And it's *Scar Man!*"

Raven floated by again and looked admiringly at her teammate. "You can say that again," she murmured.

CHAPTER 6

For the rest of the afternoon, the giant robotic Scar Man sat in the Titans Tower living room, his arms crossed and a big frown on his face. Nearby, Cyborg was yelling at him.

"You do *not* get it!" Cyborg insisted.

Scar Man shook his head and said, "Oh, I get it. I used to have little-kid arms and legs.

Now I'm bigger and manlier than ever!"

Suddenly, Robin burst into the room. He was chasing former Beast Boy's left leg, which jumped under the couch.

"Come out from there right now!" Robin commanded, bending over to search for the sneaky leg.

As he did that, former Beast Boy's right leg hopped into the room and kicked Robin in the rear, knocking him over.

Cyborg chuckled and said to Scar Man, "Okay, I have to admit that was kind of funny. But what you have done to your body is *not* an improvement!"

Robin was curled up in a ball on the floor while former Beast Boy's two feet started kicking him.

"Can I get a little help here?" he pleaded.

Meanwhile, Raven was in her room
watching her favorite TV show about
enchanted horses, *Pretty, Pretty Pegasus*,
when she felt something tug on her cloak.
She looked down and saw former Beast Boy's

left hand pulling on the edge of her cloak. The hand was holding a note, which it passed along to Raven.

Raven opened the note and read the horribly messy handwriting. It said, "I have my eye on you."

"I don't get it," Raven said as she looked down at the hand. It pointed up in the air, and when Raven looked up to the ceiling she saw former Beast Boy's disembodied left eye.

It winked at her.

"Okay, that is *so* not tough," she thought to herself. "That is just gross!"

In the Titans Tower kitchen, Robin was sitting at a table, struggling against former Beast Boy's right arm in an epic arm-wrestling battle.

"If I win, you agree to go into the cryogenic tube," the Boy Wonder said.

Just when it seemed that Robin was about to defeat former Beast Boy's arm, it transformed into a gorilla's arm and smashed Robin's hand to the table.

"Ouch!" cried Robin as former Beast Boy's triumphant arm bounced out of the kitchen.

Back in the living room, two giant music
speakers had emerged from robotic Scar
Man's shoulders. Bass-thumping disco music
now filled the room as Scar Man danced from
one robot foot to the other.

Cyborg entered the room and called out
over the loud music, "Good news, bro! I
figured out how to reattach all your body
parts!"

Scar Man closed his eyes and kept dancing.
"Can't hear you," he said to Cyborg.

"It's a simple procedure, and you'll be back
to your old self," Cyborg yelled even louder.

Scar Man shook his head and said, "No,
thanks, bro. I prefer to remain awesome.
Hey, check this out...*flame thrower*!"

Blaaaaaam!

A cannon-shaped nozzle emerged from his robotic arm and shot out a giant flame that burned a hole in the wall. As Cyborg stared at the hole in disbelief, two giant rocket boosters emerged from Scar Man's robotic feet.

"I'm taking this party sky-high!" he said and blasted up in the air, crashing through the roof.

Cyborg shook his head sadly and said, "There must be a way to make him realize that what he's done to his body is terrible!"

Just then, former Beast Boy's right arm crawled into the living room and wrapped itself around Cyborg's leg.

"Hmmm," said Cyborg. "That gives me an idea!"

CHAPTER 7

Later that day, Scar Man was standing outside Titans Tower, looking tough, blasting some tunes from his shoulder speakers and shooting lasers out of his new robot arm into the sky.

Just then, Cyborg called out to him in a sarcastic tone of voice, "Hey, Beast Boy! Look at me! Look at how tough I've made myself!"

Scar Man's one good eye widened when

he saw how his teammate had transformed himself. Cyborg had removed all his robotic body parts and replaced them with former Beast Boy's discarded body parts!

Pop!

Cyborg's new arms and legs transformed into animal parts.

"Check out these fierce gorilla arms," Cyborg said. "And how about these awesome horse haunches?"

Pop!

Cyborg's gorilla arms changed into giant crab claws.

"Ooh, crab claws!" Cyborg said as he clicked his claws together. "So tough! Do these horse legs make me manlier?"

Scar Man was shocked. "What have you done to yourself, Cyborg?" he asked.

"I'm teaching you a lesson," Cyborg replied, "that cutting off body parts and replacing them with other parts is *not* cool!"

"Uh-huh," said Scar Man, who was not convinced. "What else?"

"Taking care of yourself is way more important than looking tough, man!" Cyborg yelled.

Scar Man rolled his eye and asked, "You done yet?"

Cyborg sighed and admitted defeat. "Yeah, I guess I'm done," he said. With a sad shake of his head, he slowly turned away.

Scar Man watched as Cyborg trotted away on his horse legs. Suddenly, Scar Man felt bad that he had ignored his friend's advice. He walked over to Cyborg.

"I'm sorry, bro," said Scar Man. "I guess

I kind of got carried away in my pursuit of toughness."

Cyborg looked down at his crab claws and horse hooves. With a laugh, he said, "I think we *both* got a little carried away!"

Scar Man smiled back at his friend. "You *do* look pretty tough, though, dude!" he said.

"You really think this looks tough?" Cyborg asked.

"You just upped your tough factor five times!" Scar Man declared.

"Then let's get out of here and tough it out with a burp-off, bro!" Cyborg said as he reached up a crab claw to high-five Scar Man's robotic hand.

Later that day, Cyborg and Beast Boy

were back to their normal selves, sitting on a couch in the Titans Tower living room.

Burrrrrp! went Beast Boy.

Bellllllllch! went Cyborg.

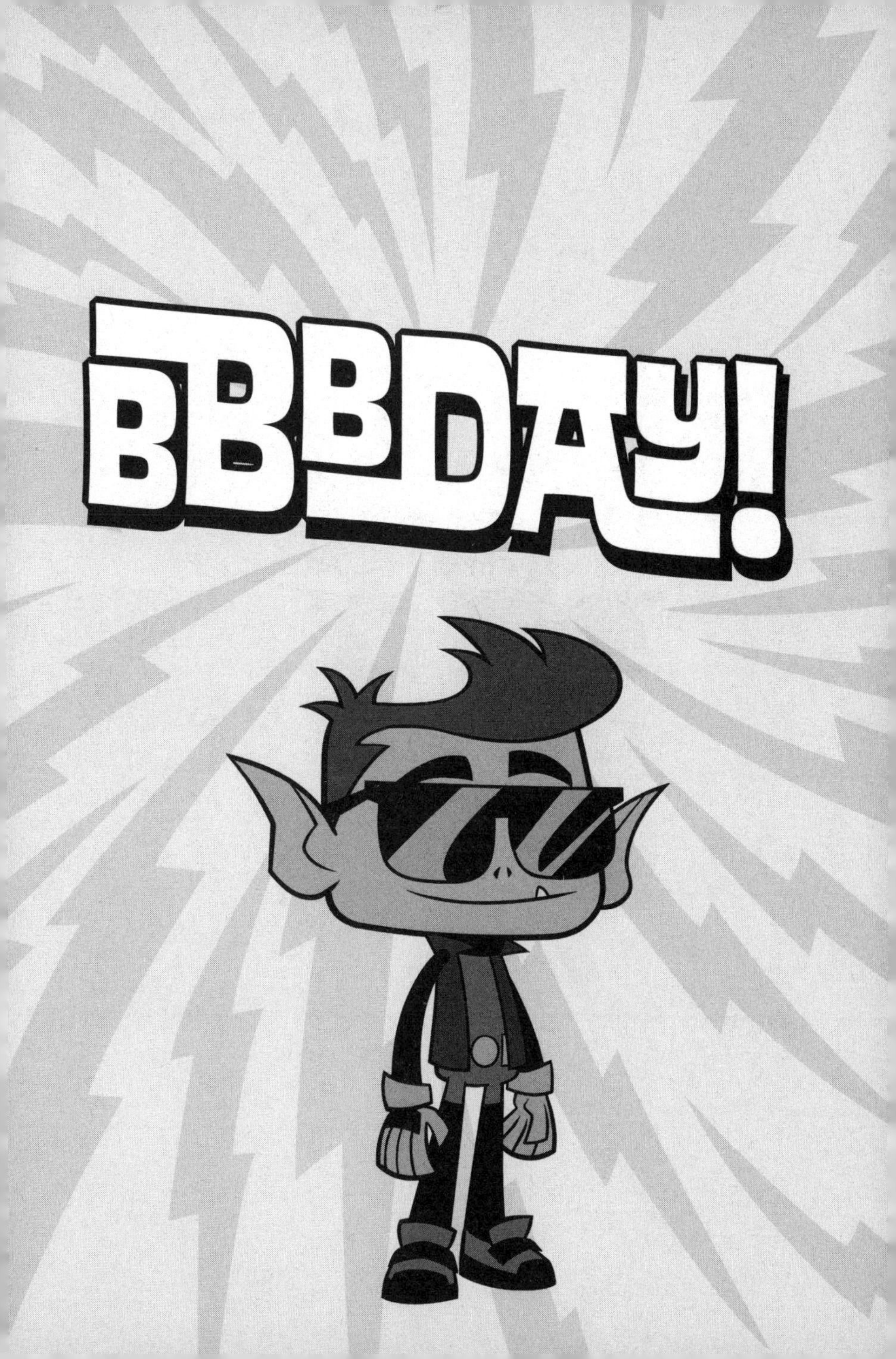
BBDAY!

CHAPTER 1

It was early Tuesday morning in Titans Tower, and Beast Boy was snoring gently in his bed as the first rays of sunshine came creeping through the blinds in his window. Suddenly, his eyes popped wide open, and a big grin filled his face. He hopped out of bed and ran to the calendar on the wall. This day on the calendar had been circled with a thick red marker. Tiny stickers with stars and cakes surrounded the date.

"Oh, yeah!" said Beast Boy. He danced from foot to foot and happily sang, *"My name is B-Boy! Today's my b-day! I'm gonna eat some yummy b-cake and score some awesome b-presents!"*

He quickly slipped on his uniform and ran a comb through his hair. Taking a look in the mirror admiringly, he said to his reflection, "Bro, today you are the *center* of the universe! Now get out there and make your friends sing you a song, watch you blow out your candles, and shower you with presents!"

Beast Boy bounced down the hall and then burst into the living room, doing his happy dance. No one looked up at him. Robin was studying a chart, Cyborg was watching TV, and both Starfire and Raven were reading.

"What's happening, everybodies!" Beast Boy called out to his teammates as he danced into the room.

Cyborg turned away from the TV screen for a moment and said, "Look at you!"

Beast Boy ran over to him and pressed his face close to Cyborg's. "Yeah, you will look at me!" Beast Boy said. "*All day long!*"

"Oooh, someone is feeling the good feelings," Starfire observed.

"That's right!" Beast Boy agreed. "Because today is my special day!"

Raven didn't even look up from her book. "What's so special about today?" she asked.

"Like you don't know," Beast Boy said with a laugh. "Now, c'mon! Let's get this party started."

Robin checked the calendar app on his phone. "There are no parties scheduled for today," he said very matter-of-factly.

Beast Boy stopped dancing for a moment, totally confused by the reaction of his teammates. Then he smiled.

"Oh, I *get* it!" he said with a grin. "You guys are doin' it surprise style. I love it! I'll just step out of the room for a moment!"

As Beast Boy bounded out of the room, Raven shook her head. "Whatever," she muttered.

Beast Boy stood in the hallway outside the living room for almost two minutes, slowly counting, "One, two...cake is in the room. Three, four, five...candles are lit. Six, seven, eight...party hats are on. Nine, ten...they're ready for me!"

He then called out in a loud voice, "I wonder what my friends could be doing now?"

With that, he charged back into the room, jumping high in the air and landing with a thud, as the Titans ignored him. Beast Boy surveyed the room with disbelief. There was no cake, and there were no presents!

"Okay, I got it," Beast Boy said as he stood

up and walked out of the room again. "You need more time to set it up. I'll be back!"

"Make it a decade," said Raven in an annoyed voice.

Thud!

Beast Boy jumped back into the living room. There was no party. He stalked out again.

Thud!

Once again, he made an appearance. Once again, he was ignored.

Thud!

He bounded into the room again.

"Will you *stop* doing that?" Robin yelled at him.

"Yeah, bro," agreed Cyborg. "We are trying to quietly enjoy our activities."

Beast Boy thought for a moment, and then he said, "Oh, man. You guys must have *really* big party plans for today!"

He then ran over to Cyborg and pried open his robotic chest plate. Beast Boy peered inside and listened as his voice echoed, "What's in there? What's in there? What's in there?"

Cyborg angrily tossed Beast Boy onto the couch, where he bumped into Raven and Starfire.

"Beastie, what the heck is wrong with you today?" Cyborg demanded.

"I thought maybe you had something for me inside there," Beast Boy explained. "You know, something that's square, with colorful wrapping paper, and maybe a big red bow. You know what I'm saying?"

Cyborg shook his head with dismay. "You're freaking me out, dude," he said.

Wee-o! Wee-o!

Suddenly, the Titans Tower crime siren started wailing. Robin ran to the computer.

"Crime alert!" he called to his teammates.

Beast Boy sat on the couch while the other Titans jumped into action.

"*Good* cover," he said with a smile. "Does this 'crime alert' involve cake and wrapping paper?"

"No!" said Robin with exasperation. "There's a herd of elephants on a crime spree downtown!"

Beast Boy winked at Robin and said, "*Right,* dude! While you guys take care of those criminal elephants, I'll wait here ready to be surprised."

Raven looked at Beast Boy and shook her head. "Whatever," she said.

"Titans, go!" called out Robin as the others rushed out of the Titans Tower.

Beast Boy sat back on the couch and folded his arms, a satisfied smile on his face. He was content to wait.

As the day dragged on, and his friends failed to return to the Tower, Beast Boy smiled and waited.

When the sun started to go down, Beast Boy was still alone, sitting in the dark, smiling and waiting.

When the clock struck 11:00 p.m. and there was still no party, Beast Boy jumped off the couch and stalked into the kitchen. He was no longer smiling.

CHAPTER 2

"What a great party, bros!" Beast Boy said with a laugh. "And now it's time for you to watch me open my presents."

Beast Boy was sitting at the kitchen table, wearing a brightly colored party hat. Surrounding him were some of his favorite stuffed animals, one in each kitchen chair.

Beast Boy lifted a stuffed giraffe and pried open its mouth, pretending that the giraffe was excitedly talking to him and laughing.

"Today is all about you, Beast Boy!" he said in a squeaky voice as he wiggled the stuffed giraffe's mouth.

Beast Boy then reached for a box of cereal and ripped it open, spilling a handful of flakes into his hand.

"Oh, wow!" he said as he popped the cereal into his mouth. "So thoughtful!"

He then grabbed a stuffed crocodile and opened its mouth.

"Open my present next!" he said in a gruff voice.

Just as Beast Boy was opening a box of dried pasta, his teammates entered the kitchen. They stared at the scene before them with disbelief.

"Bro, what are you *doing*?" asked Cyborg.

Beast Boy glared at the Titans and said in

a sulky voice, "I'm just enjoying my birthday since my real friends forgot! Want some cake?"

With that, he offered Cyborg a chunk of swiss cheese that had a small candle in it.

"We did not do the forgetting," Starfire

gently explained to Beast Boy. "We knew it was your birthday."

Beast Boy was astonished. "Then why didn't you treat me like I'm the center of the universe?" he demanded.

Robin put his hand on Beast Boy's shoulder and leaned in to explain, "Because other people's birthdays are so boring! Awkwardly singing that birthday song…"

"And the eating of the birthday cake with the spittle and candle wax upon it," added Starfire. "Yuck!"

"Watching gifts being opened and pretending to care," said Cyborg with a yawn.

Beast Boy frowned and said, "Dudes, I'm sorry my birthday is such a bummer for you, but it's nice to have one day a year when all the attention is on *me*!"

Raven looked worried. "I totally forgot it was your birthday," she said. "You should have told me!"

Beast Boy smiled and put his arms around Raven, giving her a tight hug. "Thanks, Rae-Rae. You're the only one who really cares about me!"

Blam!

Raven knocked Beast Boy to the ground and said, "I *don't* care about you! But there are cosmic consequences to forgetting someone's birthday. What time is it?"

Cyborg flipped open his chest plate to reveal a digital clock. "It's 11:59 p.m.," he said.

"Almost midnight!" Raven said frantically. "We have one minute to shower Beast Boy with attention before the day is over!"

She looked at Beast Boy's party hat and the torn boxes of cereal and pasta on the table.

"Okay, he has presents," she said. "We just need to sing to him! Everybody, c'mon…"

Beast Boy smiled as his teammates began to sing to him, "*Happy birthday to...*"

Clong!

Cyborg's digital clock chimed when midnight arrived.

"Nooooooo!" screamed Raven.

Her teammates looked confused. "What's the big deal, Raven?" asked Cyborg.

"*That* is the big deal," said Raven as she pointed to Beast Boy, who, at the stroke of midnight, had been transformed into a small infant wearing a diaper.

"Waaaaaah!" cried baby Beast Boy.

CHAPTER 3

The next day, the Titans gathered in their living room. Baby Beast Boy was still crying, just as he had done all night long. None of his teammates had gotten a good night's sleep, and they were all tired.

With a yawn, Starfire walked over to Beast Boy and picked him up. He finally stopped crying, and she said, "Who is the good Beast Baby? *You* are the good Beast Baby!"

Cyborg turned to Raven. "So Beast Boy is a baby because we didn't celebrate his birthday?" he asked skeptically.

"When we go to birthday parties and just stare at the person while they eat cake and open presents, we create time anchors," Raven explained. "This allows the person to grow old naturally. Without those time anchors, the universe has no idea how old you are. You can see the disastrous results for yourself!"

"That's messed up," said Cyborg. As he looked at Beast Boy, Cyborg let out a yelp and said, "Whoa! That's even more messed up!"

The Titans turned to stare at Beast Boy and were astonished to see that he had transformed into a little old man.

"Did I ever tell you kids about the time I had to walk to school through eight feet of snow?" he said in a scratchy voice.

"Eeek!" said Starfire as she dropped senior Beast Boy on the floor.

Robin pondered the situation. "There must be something we can do to fix him!" he said.

Raven sighed and said, "Well, there is one way to save him. We need to celebrate his

birthday at the center of the universe."

Starfire, Robin, and Cyborg all gasped. Beast Boy coughed and said, "In my day, a quarter bought you a comic book and candy, and you still got some change back!"

"The journey to the center of the universe

is perilous," said Raven. "We may not make it back."

Cyborg looked at Beast Boy, who was now walking across the room using a cane.

"Well, maybe he's not *so* bad this way," Cyborg said reluctantly.

"The baby Beast Boy is adorable," agreed Starfire. "And the senior Beast Boy has wonderful stories."

Raven turned serious. "You are all forgetting…middle age!" she warned.

They all looked at Beast Boy, who suddenly transformed into a middle-aged man with a giant gut that popped open the buttons on his shirt.

Middle-aged Beast Boy sighed. "Would you look at the time? I'm going to be late for work," he said as he ran a comb through his hair, stretching four greasy strands of hair in a futile attempt to cover up a bald spot at the top of his head.

"Yuck," said Robin. "Okay, Raven. Lead the way!"

CHAPTER 4

In the middle of the Titans Tower living room, Raven magically opened a portal that led to the center of the universe. One by one, the Titans stepped through the portal, then the door slammed behind them. What they saw on the other side of the door astonished them.

The Titans were floating through outer space, but there were no stars or planets around them. Instead, giant birthday items surrounded them. A frosted angel food cake floated by. A box covered in gift wrap bumped into Cyborg. An immense birthday sparkler suddenly materialized, set itself on fire, and started sending off sparks.

"Welcome to the center of the universe," said Raven. "This is where everyone wants to be on his or her birthday."

Starfire gasped. "Oooh, it is very festive!"

"Don't let the birthday goodies fool you," cautioned Raven. "This place is actually super-boring. If we don't complete all the birthday rituals before that sparkler burns down, we'll be stuck here forever. And we'll have to clean up after the party, too!"

"Clean up?" Robin shrieked. "We can't let that happen!"

"I really should be heading to my office now," said middle-aged Beast Boy as he carefully placed a sandwich into his briefcase. "I've used up all my vacation days...."

"There's no time to lose!" said Robin. "He's stuck in middle age!"

Pop!

A giant chair suddenly materialized under

Beast Boy, and a table covered with birthday presents appeared in front of him.

"Let's get this party started with the most important part—the song!" said Cyborg, who started singing, "*Happy birthday to…*"

"No!" yelled Raven. "It is a violation of the intergalactic copyright laws to sing that song in outer space. We'll need to make up a new birthday song."

"How hard can that be?" said Cyborg. After pondering a moment, he started singing, "*Hey, you, great job being born. You stayed alive again this year.…*"

Robin joined in, "*La la la la, you are the amazing birthday person.…*"

Starfire finished the song by adding, "*The cake with too much frosting will be enjoyed by all.*"

There was a moment of silence before Cyborg asked, "Did it work?"

Blam!

Confetti erupted around the Titans. A new door suddenly appeared, and the Titans cautiously walked through it. The burning sparkler followed behind them.

"We have successfully completed part one," said Raven.

"Would somebody please call my office and let them know that I'm going to be late?" grumbled middle-aged Beast Boy.

CHAPTER 5

When the Titans stepped through the next door, they discovered a three-layer birthday cake that had two burning candles and the frosted initials *BB* on top.

Pop!

Beast Boy now became a two-year-old, sitting in a highchair and reaching out his tiny hands to grab the cake.

"For this next ritual, we have to take a

good picture of Beast Boy in front of his cake and then watch as he blows out his birthday candles," said Raven.

"How is the adorable baby Beast Boy supposed to blow out candles?" asked Starfire with concern.

"Yeah, he doesn't have the lung capacity yet," said Cyborg.

"And he's too young to even know what's going on!" added Robin.

Raven nodded wearily. "I agree that it's all pointless, but it's the rule. We have no choice."

Robin grabbed a camera that was floating nearby.

"Beast Boy!" he called. "Beast Boy, look over here! Hey, look at the camera! Be a good boy!"

Beast Boy looked up, down, sideways, and behind him. He looked everywhere but at Robin.

"He won't look at me," Robin said with a frown. "Hey, guys, help me get his attention."

Cyborg popped his head off his body and then tossed it from hand to hand in an attempt to get Beast Boy's attention. Starfire flipped upside down and began executing perfect somersaults. Raven opened her mouth as wide as possible until it covered her entire face and then stuck out her tongue.

Beast Boy started to turn his head to look at the Titans, but then he got distracted by the cake and jammed one hand into the gooey frosting.

"We almost got him," Robin called out. "Titans, go funnier!"

Cyborg dislocated all his body parts. Starfire started spinning so fast that soon she was just a blur of motion. Raven's tongue became bigger than her whole body, and she shouted funny noises.

It worked! Beast Boy looked up at his teammates and smiled.

Click!

Robin snapped an adorable picture of baby

Beast Boy with a big smile on his face.

"Okay, now he needs to blow out his birthday candles," said Raven.

Starfire floated over to Beast Boy and put an encouraging hand on his shoulder.

"Can you make the blowing out for Starfire?" she asked gently. "Yes, you can! Yes, you can!"

Beast Boy drew in his breath, exhaled, and then gently drooled on his two candles.

"Ewww," said Cyborg. "A cake covered in baby spit and candle wax. I think I'll pass!"

Beast Boy was determined to blow out his candles. He inhaled as deeply as he could, puffed out his cheeks as far as he could, opened his mouth as wide as he could, and shot a mighty stream of drool onto the candles. They both went out!

"He did it!" yelled Cyborg happily. "It was disgusting, but he did it!"

Blam!

The Titans were showered with confetti again, and a new open door appeared.

"The birthday sparkler is dangerously low," said Raven, "and we still have one final birthday ritual that awaits us through this next portal."

"And who is going to carry the drooling baby?" Cyborg asked, but no one answered. All his other teammates had already hurried through the door.

Cyborg reluctantly picked up the gurgling baby Beast Boy.

"Cool it with the drool, okay, bro?" he implored. "Some of us rust when we get wet!"

CHAPTER 6

After they passed through the portal, Raven gathered everyone around a large box that was covered in birthday wrapping paper with a shiny red bow on top.

"Our final birthday ritual is to watch Beast Boy open a present and pretend to be interested," she said.

"That's easy!" declared Robin.

"Don't get too cocky," cautioned Raven. "It's harder than you think."

"A present for me? You shouldn't have," said Beast Boy, who had changed into a senior citizen again as he traveled through the portal. "So thoughtful. So considerate."

Beast Boy slowly shuffled over to the present. As he paused to look it over, Raven looked nervously at the dwindling sparkler.

"I'll just peel back the tape so that we can save this beautiful wrapping paper," Beast Boy said as he worked one fingernail under a seam of the gift wrap. "As I always say, waste not, want not...."

"C'mon, Grandpa, move it along!" yelled Robin. "There's no time for this!"

Starfire looked dismayed. "He is taking all four of the evers!"

Beast Boy continued to gently tug at the wrapping paper. "Haste makes waste," he said slowly.

"Open it already!" screamed Cyborg.

Raven glared at her teammates. "Remember, we have to *enjoy* this!" she told them.

Robin was dismayed. "How can I enjoy this when the present isn't for me?" he asked.

Raven sighed. "Can you at least smile awkwardly?" she asked.

All four Titans put fixed grins on their faces as they watched Beast Boy slowly...very slowly...unwrap his present. Finally, Beast Boy reached into the box and pulled out a pair of socks.

Robin kept the grin on his face. "Wow, how great is that? Socks!" he said through clenched teeth.

"What an exciting gift," said Starfire not too convincingly.

"And I bet they are one hundred percent cotton," said Cyborg without much enthusiasm.

Blam!

Confetti again poured down onto the Titans, and a new door magically appeared.

As his teammates watched in astonishment, Beast Boy rapidly transformed through a dozen different ages, from cooing newborn to surly teenager to cranky oldster. In his final transformation, he became the one-and-only Teen Titan they all knew.

"We did it!" yelled Raven, who cast a nervous look back at the sparkler. "Everyone through the door before the sparkler burns out. Come on!"

Thinking fast, Beast Boy grabbed his birthday cake. Then he and his teammates jumped through the portal just as the sparkler burned out. The Titans all landed together with a thud in their living room.

Raven turned to Beast Boy and said, "Sorry I forgot your birthday, Beast Boy."

"And the rest of us are sorry that we

intentionally ignored it," added Starfire.

"Yeah, we had no idea it was so important to stare at you all day and pretend to care about you," admitted Robin.

"It's cool," said Beast Boy as he lifted a knife to slice into his birthday cake. "Now let's eat this yummy cake!"

Cyborg looked doubtful. "Um, is that the same cake that was covered with baby spit and melted candle wax?"

"Oh, yeah!" said Beast Boy as he placed the first slice on a plate. "Who's ready for cake?"

No one answered. Beast Boy looked up and was surprised to see that he was alone.

"That's weird," said Beast Boy. "I thought they liked cake. Oh well. More for me! "

After he gobbled down his first slice of cake, Beast Boy burped and said happily,

"Best birthday ever! And just think, only three hundred sixty-three days until my *next* birthday!"

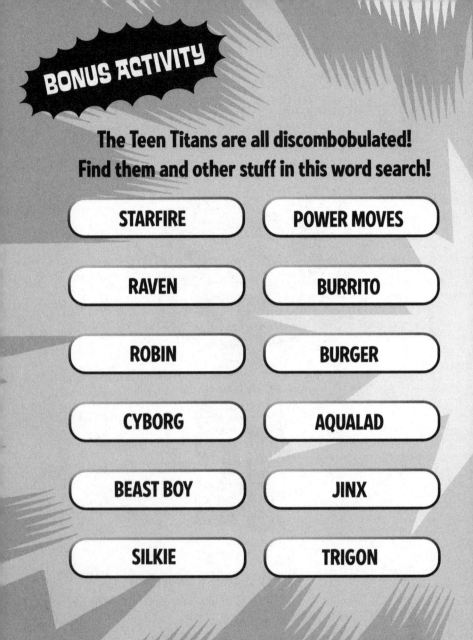

BONUS ACTIVITY

The Teen Titans are all discombobulated!
Find them and other stuff in this word search!

STARFIRE	POWER MOVES
RAVEN	BURRITO
ROBIN	BURGER
CYBORG	AQUALAD
BEAST BOY	JINX
SILKIE	TRIGON

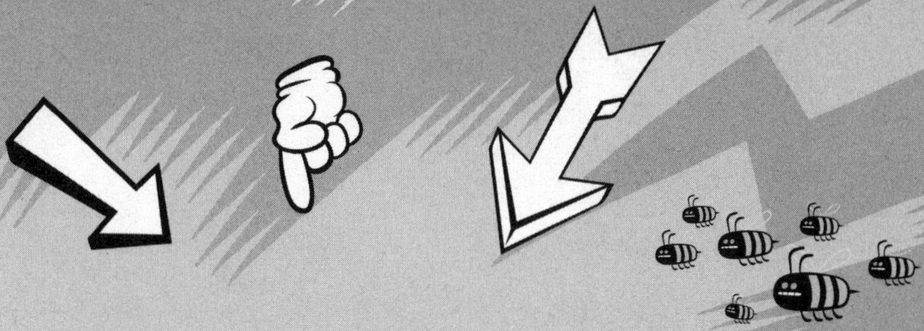

P	E	R	E	G	R	U	B	E	Y
O	R	L	G	T	B	X	I	R	D
W	I	Y	B	T	R	K	N	Y	B
E	F	D	R	U	L	I	O	I	G
R	R	D	A	I	R	B	G	R	J
M	A	N	S	L	T	R	O	O	R
O	T	R	E	S	A	B	I	O	N
V	S	M	A	V	Y	U	B	T	K
E	N	E	L	C	A	I	Q	G	O
S	B	Y	M	R	N	R	L	A	R

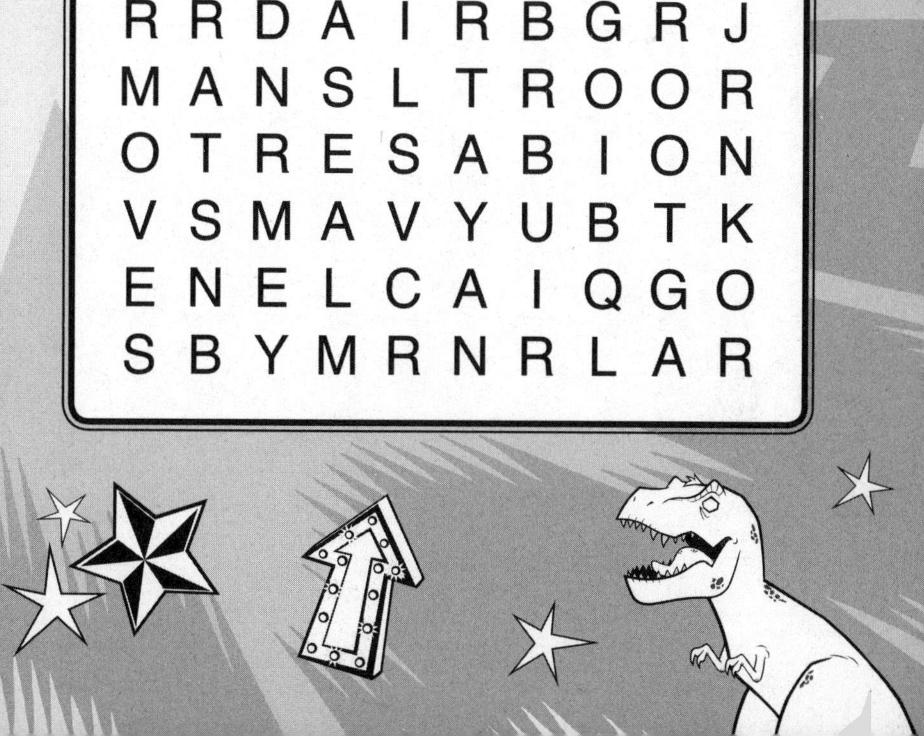

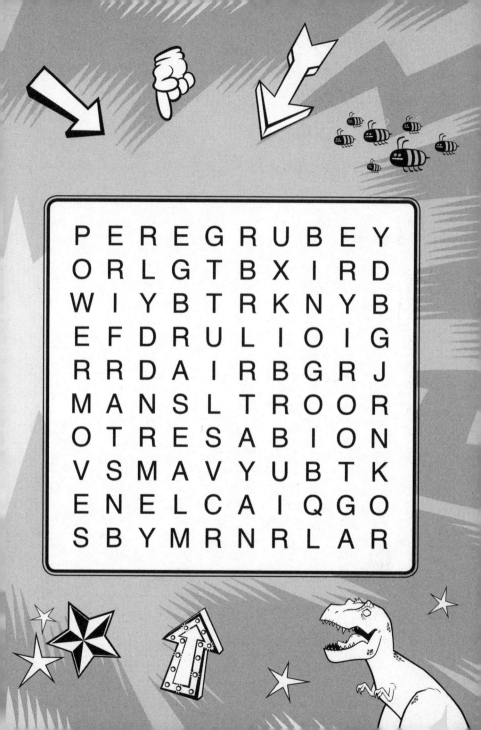

Don't miss these
TEEN TITANS GO! books.